This book belongs to

_____

For James MC-M

For my family and friends CC

Text copyright © 1993 Marita Conlon-McKenna
Illustrations copyright © 1993 Christopher Coady

First published in Ireland 1993 by The O'Brien Press Ltd.
20 Victoria Road, Dublin 6, Ireland
Originally published in 1993 by ABC, All Books for Children,
a division of the All Children's Company Ltd
33 Museum Street, London WC1A 1LD

Printed and bound in Hong Kong

British Library Cataloguing in Publication Data
Conlon-McKenna, Marita
Little Star
I. Title II. Coady, Christopher
823.914

ISBN 0-86278-348-8

Little Star

written by
**Marita
Conlon-McKenna**

illustrated by
**Christopher
Coady**

THE O'BRIEN PRESS

DUBLIN

The little star hovered over hot sandy deserts and high snow-topped mountains. It gleamed over dark forests of green pines and winked at the ocean waves. It sparkled over city streets.

And then that night the star fell and fell until it landed in a patch of weeds at the bottom of a garden.

"James! Time to come in!"

There were dark shadows everywhere.
James dodged and ran through them.

Then something twinkled and caught his eye.
He bent down and touched it. "Ouch!" It was
hot, and felt rough and sharp. He turned it
over but he couldn't figure out what it was.

"James!"

"Coming!"

James hid the sparkling shape in his jacket, raced up
to his room and put it with his collection of treasures.
Soon it was time for his goodnight story. James
closed his eyes. Then Mum went downstairs, clicking
off the light as she left.

James sat up in bed. He had been asleep.
"It must be the middle of the night," he thought.
He could hear the clock ticking on the landing.
His light was off, but there was a glow coming
from his shelf in the corner of the room. James
got up and went to look.

His shape was winking and twinkling.
"Oh!" he cried. "You're a star!"

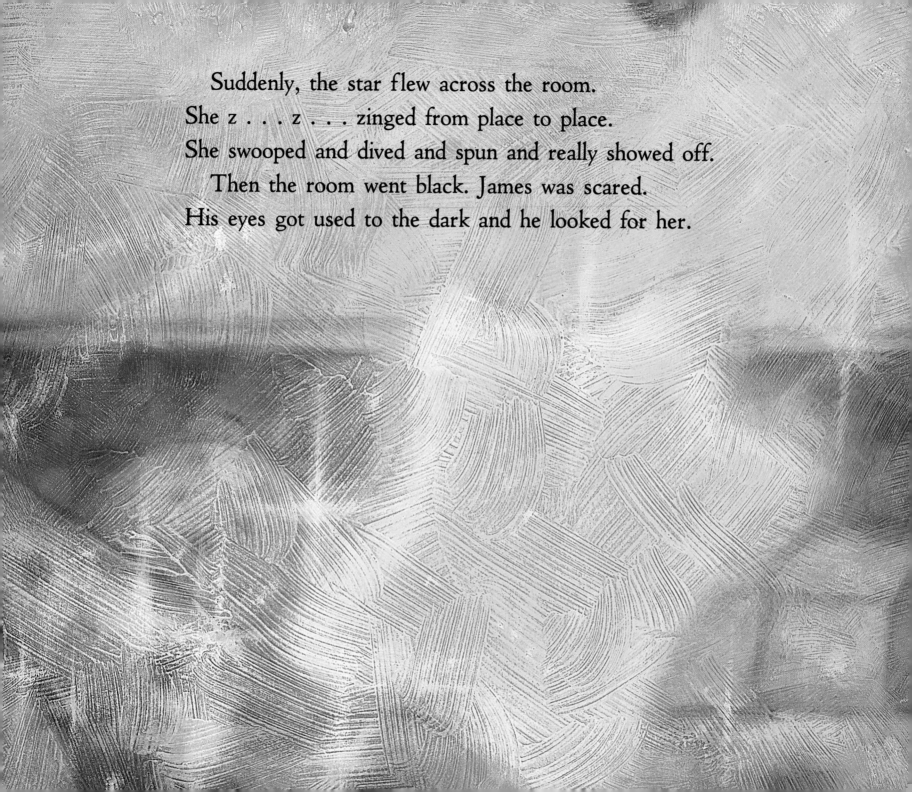

Suddenly, the star flew across the room.

She z . . . z . . . zinged from place to place.

She swooped and dived and spun and really showed off.

Then the room went black. James was scared.

His eyes got used to the dark and he looked for her.

She was hiding under his bed!

"Star!" he called. She jumped out, then disappeared again. James found her in his toy box.

"So that's it," laughed James. "Hide and seek!" And they played until James grew tired and went back to bed.

The next morning, James whispered, "Hello," but when he touched her, she felt cooler and hard.

James could hardly wait for night to come. And again, the star twirled around the room. But, this time, she didn't want to hide. James thought she was looking for something. "Do you want to see my toys?" he asked, and emptied his toy box. All his cars lay spread out on the carpet.

But the star seemed bored.
Then James thought of
something. "This is my farm set!
It's my very best toy!"

One by one, he lifted up the animals and showed them
to the star: the cow, the pigs, the big horse and the sheep.
She seemed to recognise them, and lit each one in turn.
James yawned. "I'll clean up in the morning," he said.
The star watched over them all as he slept.

On the third night, the star stopped in front of the window.
James was tired and stayed in bed. "Would you like to see my
books?" he asked. "This is about a boy called Jack who climbed
up a giant beanstalk." As he turned the pages, the star rested on
his pillow. Her light flickered, like a flashlight growing dim and
James's skin no longer felt hot when she was near. His eyes closed.
The book slipped from his hands and he was asleep.

The next day when James went to say good morning to the star, she lay still. Glittering dust scattered the shelf and clung to the birds' feathers — she was crumbling away.

He touched her gently with his fingertips. She was almost cold, and felt brittle and rough. His star was dying! Soon there would be nothing left but shiny dust.

"Oh, star!" he whispered.

That night, he put the star in
his jacket and carried her out to the
garden. All around was darkness.

"Goodbye, little star," he whispered.

And, with one huge stretch, he
flung the star as far as he could into
the blackness.

Then he turned and ran inside
without looking back.

That night his bedroom seemed lonely, and his
treasure shelf looked dull.
"You don't even need the light tonight," Mum said,
"it's so bright from the stars."
James pressed his face against the window.
High above, the little star flashed
and danced and twinkled
. . . just for James.